Katie Woo

Katie's Happy Mother's Day

by Fran Manushkin

illustrated by Tammie Lyon

PICTURE WINDOW BOOKS
a capstone imprint

Katie Woo is published by Picture Window Books,
A Capstone Imprint
1710 Roe Crest Drive
North Mankato, Minnesota 56003
www.capstonepub.com

Library of Congress Cataloging-in-Publication Data
Manushkin, Fran, author.
  Katie's happy Mother's Day / by Fran Manushkin; illustrated by Tammie Lyon.
      pages cm -— (Katie Woo)
  Summary: When Katie's mother feels unwell on the day before Mother's Day, Katie wants to do everything she can think of to help her mother get well—but she forgot to get a present.
  ISBN 978-1-4795-6179-7 (library binding) — ISBN 978-1-4795-6181-0 (paperback.) — ISBN 978-1-4795-6190-2 (eBook pdf)
1. Woo, Katie (Fictitious character)—Juvenile fiction. 2. Chinese Americans—Juvenile fiction. 3. Mother's Day—Juvenile fiction. 4. Helping behavior—Juvenile fiction. 5. Mothers and daughters—Juvenile fiction. [1. Chinese Americans—Fiction. 2. Mother's Day—Fiction. 3. Gifts—Fiction. 4. Helpfulness—Fiction.] I. Lyon, Tammie, illustrator. II. Title. III. Series: Manushkin, Fran. Katie Woo.
  PZ7.M3195Kc 2015
  813.54—dc23
  [E]   2014041796

Graphic Designer: Kristi Carlson

Photo Credits:
Greg Holch, pg. 26
Tammie Lyon, pg. 26

Printed in the United States of America in North Mankato, Minnesota
032015   008823CGF15

Table of Contents

Chapter 1

Taking Care of Mom

It was Saturday morning.

Katie was eating pancakes.

But her mom was not eating.

"What's wrong?" Katie

asked her mom.

"I don't feel well," she said.

"Maybe you should go back to bed," said Katie. "That's what I did when I had the flu."

"I think I will," said her mom.

"I will fluff up your pillow

and tuck you in," said Katie.

"This is cozy." Her mom

smiled. "If I sleep for a while,

I'll feel better."

"Take my Teddy," offered

Katie. "When I hold Teddy,

he helps me sleep."

Katie's mom hugged

Teddy tight.

Katie pulled down the

shades, saying, "Bye-bye, sun.

Mom needs to sleep now."

Katie's mom began to yawn. "I am feeling sleepy," she said.

"Good," said Katie. "I'll sing you a lullaby."

Katie sang, "Sleep, sleep, go to sleep. Dream of fluffy little sheep. You'll feel better when you wake — no more head or belly ache."

The lullaby worked! Katie's
mom fell asleep. Katie tiptoed
out of the room.

She called
JoJo and told
her, "My mom
is sick."

"Oh, no!" said JoJo.

"Tomorrow is Mother's Day. I

hope she's okay by then."

Chapter 2

Uh-oh!

When Katie's mom woke up, she looked a lot better.

"My headache is almost gone," she said. "You and Teddy and the nap really helped."

"Now you will have a happy Mother's Day," said Katie.

But *Uh-oh!* thought Katie. *I don't have a Mother's Day present for Mom.*

Katie's dad told Katie, "I got Mom a necklace. It can be from both of us."

"Thanks," said Katie. "But I want to give Mom something on my own."

Katie called
Pedro and
asked him
what to do.

He told
Katie, "Why
don't you make a card?"

"I'll paint a red one," said
Katie. "Red is Mom's favorite
color. But I want to give her
a nice present too."

"I could give her flowers from our garden," said Katie. "She loves red roses. But none of them are blooming."

That night, Katie dreamed

that she painted the house

red. Her mother loved it!

But it was only a dream.

Chapter 3

A Mother's Day Surprise

When Katie woke up, she felt sad. She didn't want to tell her mom, "I forgot to get you a gift."

But before Katie could say it, her mom said, "I have a surprise for you."

She gave Katie a pretty

card. It said:

I'm the happiest mom

that I can be!

Katie is the girl for me.

She is great in every way.

Every day is Mother's Day!

"I'm so happy!" said Katie.

"Me too!" said her mom, wiggling her toes.

"Aha!" said Katie. "Now I know what to give you — a pedicure!"

Katie painted her mother's

toes a bright, happy red.

"Wow!" said her mom.

"My toes and I thank you!"

Katie's grandma came over, and she got a pedicure too.

"Our daughters are the best," said Katie's mom and grandmother.

It was a very happy day!

About the Author

Fran Manushkin is the author of many popular picture books, including *Baby, Come Out!*; *Latkes and Applesauce: A Hanukkah Story*; *The Tushy Book*; *The Belly Book*; and *Big Girl Panties*. There is a real Katie Woo — she's Fran's great-niece — but she never gets in half the trouble of the Katie Woo in the books. Fran writes on her beloved Mac computer in New York City, without the help of her two naughty cats, Chaim and Goldy.

About the Illustrator

Tammie Lyon began her love for drawing at a young age while sitting at the kitchen table with her dad. She continued her love of art and eventually attended the Columbus College of Art and Design, where she earned a bachelor's degree in fine art. After a brief career as a professional ballet dancer, she decided to devote herself full time to illustration. Today she lives with her husband, Lee, in Cincinnati, Ohio. Her dogs, Gus and Dudley, keep her company as she works in her studio.

Glossary

ache (AKE)—a dull pain that goes on and on

blooming (BLOOM-ing)—producing flowers

headache (HED-ake)—a pain in your head

pedicure (PED-ih-kyur)—care of the feet, toes, and toenails, often including painting the toenails

yawn (YAWN)—to open the mouth wide and to breathe in deeply, often because you are tired or bored

Discussion Questions

1. What was Katie's problem in the story, and how did she solve it? What other ways could she have solved her problem?

2. What are some of the ways Katie took care of her mom when she was sick? Did any of the things she did surprise you?

3. At the end of the book, Katie did something nice for her mom. What is the nicest thing you have ever done for someone you love?

Writing Prompts

1. Make a card for your mom or another special person in your life. Be sure to tell him or her why he or she is special to you.

2. In the story, Katie lists a few things that her mom loves. Make a list of five things that your mom loves.

3. Imagine you could give your mom anything you dreamed up for Mother's Day. Write a paragraph about what you would give her.

Having Fun with Katie Woo!

Pedicures make moms feel loved and glamorous. Give your mom this special treatment! Here's how to do a basic pedicure at home:

Pretty Pedicures

What you need:

- Footbath or large bowl
- Bubble bath
- Towel
- Lotion
- Fingernail polish

What you do:

1. Fill the footbath with warm water and a little bubble bath. Place it on the floor in front of a comfortable chair with a towel nearby. (Ask for help if it is too heavy for you.)

2. Ask your mom to sit down and soak her feet for five to ten minutes. When she's done soaking, carefully dry each foot with the towel.

3. Rub a small amount of lotion on each foot and around the ankles. Give her feet a little massage for extra special treatment.

4. Carefully paint each toe with the fingernail polish. Your mom should stay sitting for at least five minutes, to give her toes time to dry. Give her a magazine and something yummy to drink to keep her relaxed while she waits. She'll thank you for it!

THE FUN DOESN'T STOP HERE!

Discover more at www.capstonekids.com

- ♥ Videos & Contests
- ✿ Games & Puzzles
- ♥ Friends & Favorites
- ✿ Authors & Illustrators

Find cool websites and more books like this one at www.facthound.com. Just type in the Book ID: **9781479561797** and you're ready to go!